I0520305

The Meltdown Match

The Meltdown Match

USA Today Bestselling Author
RACHAEL ANDERSON

HEA Publishing

© 2015 Rachael Anderson
All rights reserved.

No part of this book may be reproduced in any form whatsoever, whether
by graphic, visual, electronic, film, microfilm, tape recording, or any other
means, without prior written permission of the publisher, except in the
case of brief passages embodied in critical reviews and articles.

This is a work of fiction. The characters, names, incidents, places, and
dialogue are products of the author's imagination, and are not to be
construed as real. The opinions and views expressed herein belong solely
to the author and do not necessarily represent the opinions or views of
HEA Publishing, LLC. Permission for the use of sources, graphics, and
photos is also solely the responsibility of the author.

ISBN: 978-1-941363-12-6

Published by HEA Publishing

For my beautiful, talented,
and only slightly superstitious niece, Courtney.
I love you, girl.

One

T he air smelled woodsy and fresh, exactly how Courtney remembered. A light breeze tickled her face as she walked. This was exactly why she loved coming home— to smell this smell and feel the wild, untamed feeling that made Heimel, Alaska the perfect place to return to for the summer.

And only for the summer.

An uncomfortable pit settled in Courtney's stomach, the same way it did every time she thought of leaving again in a few months. Would she ever be able to stay?

Hannah's arm nudged hers as they headed down Main Street, sipping strawberry smoothies. "Glad to have you back, sis, even if it's only for the summer." She sucked the last of her smoothie with a slurp. "Where next? Oregon? South Dakota? What about Canada? You haven't been out of the country yet."

"Who knows?" Courtney shrugged. "It all depends on the setting of my next book. Which is why I'm here—to get inspired. And to catch up with my favorite sister, of course."

"How nice to be an afterthought," Hannah said dryly.

Courtney laughed. "I didn't mean it like that."

"Yeah, yeah." Hannah swished her long, ebony hair behind her shoulder and lifted her face to the sun. "If you feel so inspired here, why not move back for good?"

It was a question Courtney had asked herself many times, but as much as she'd love to move back, she couldn't. It would ruin everything. She sipped the last of her smoothie then tossed the empty cup in a nearby trashcan.

Hannah would laugh and call her superstitious, but each of Courtney's four published, and two soon-to-be published books were born in Heimel—but not until *after* she'd left and returned.

The feeling of coming home was like magic, permeating her soul and leaving her rejuvenated. In only a matter of months, she could outline a story and pound out a rough draft. It was like gliding through the skies and seeing everything stretch beneath her in a large and beautiful, interconnecting pattern. But eventually, she'd inevitably find herself back on the ground, completely uninspired.

So Courtney had developed a foolproof system to keep her writing going strong: Return to Heimel, outline and write a rough draft, and move to the place where the book was set for research and revisions. Several months later, after she'd handed over the completed manuscript to her agent, she'd return to Heimel and start the process all over again.

Although moving around was exhausting, Courtney had lived in New York, Virginia, Texas, Colorado, Maine, and, most recently, California. She'd met different people, experienced new cultures, and had become a better writer. But every time she came home, Courtney couldn't help but look around with a feeling of longing, wishing things could be different and she could finally stay put. What she'd once considered an adventurous life was getting old.

With a sigh, Courtney pulled a leaf off a nearby bush and ran her fingers across the smooth, silky surface. "Maybe someday I'll move back for good. Just not yet."

"I'll believe it when I see it." Hannah stopped to look at a banner that spanned the road in front of them and pointed. "Hey, you're going to be here for the Solstice Days this year."

"So?"

She turned to Courtney, and a slow, almost devious, smile spread across her face. "So . . . that means we can both enter The Meltdown Match."

Courtney shook her head. "No way. That contest screams desperation, and I'm not desperate. Neither are you. Don't you already have a date lined up for Friday?"

"And Saturday." Hannah grinned. "But who cares? This isn't about looking desperate. It's about doing something spontaneous and having fun." She grabbed Courtney's arm, tugging her along, and Courtney's gaze dropped from the banner to the empty field across the street, where a moose stood grazing—the first moose she'd seen since her return. A sign.

Courtney smiled. Truth be known, she'd always thought of The Meltdown Match as a romantic, even magical, tradition. The so-called legend stated that on the day when the sun shined the longest, two unsuspecting hearts would be brought together in a union created by the universe. And if they later they married under the solstice sun, they were promised a lifetime of happiness.

Or something like that.

Every year during Heimel's Solstice Days, on the morning of June 21, the first official day of summer and the longest day of the year, hundreds of vases made of ice, each holding a stick with the name of a man or woman between the ages of twenty-one and twenty-nine, were left to melt in the warm summer sun. The first male and female sticks to fall were then matched for a date.

For Courtney, writer of romances with a magical twist, it sounded like a novel-worthy beginning to a wonderful love story. Who wouldn't want to say they were matched by the greatest source of light? She'd always wanted to enter the contest and win, but one thing held her back. What if her vase didn't melt first? What became of all the names the sun didn't recognize as worthy of true love? She didn't want to find out.

Granted, only a handful of the matches had ever ended in a lasting union, but a part of her couldn't help believe that the sun didn't make mistakes—only people did.

Lost in her thoughts, Courtney didn't realize where they were headed until Hannah opened a door and pulled her inside the musty-smelling city office building. Courtney immediately planted her feet and tried to tug her hand free.

"Are you deaf? I told you, I'm not entering the contest."

"Are too," Hannah countered.

"Are not."

"Too."

"Not."

"Well if it isn't Salt and Pepper arguing in public," said a deep voice behind Courtney. "Some things never change."

Courtney grinned as she turned around to meet Mitch Winter's teasing eyes. Only a few years older and a good friend, he'd made a habit of giving Courtney a hard time over the years.

"We hardly ever argue, especially in public," said Courtney. "You just have bad timing."

Mitch chuckled as he engulfed her into one of his

signature hugs, making Courtney feel warm, cozy, and more than content to stay there forever. Yet another reason she liked leaving and coming home. Mitch only hugged her like this when she came back.

"Welcome home," he said.

Courtney breathed in the clean, outdoorsy scent that always seemed to surround him. Not for the first time, she found herself wishing she were Mitch's type—willowy, classy, and a brunette—not average and blonde, something he loved to point out with the annoying nickname he'd given her of "Salt."

She reluctantly pulled free and studied his handsome, mischievous face. Green eyes. Dark, curly hair that hung just over his ears. A teasing smile that often taunted her. She slugged him lightly on his arm. "What's it going to take to get you to stop using those awful nicknames? Dying our hair?"

"Speak for yourself," Hannah said. "My hair rocks, and I like being called Pepper."

Mitch tugged on a lock of Courtney's straight, blonde hair. "Dye it red, and I'll start calling you cinnamon instead. But I like Salt better, so I hope you'll leave it alone."

"Someday I'm going to think of an equally lousy nickname for you, and you're going to rue the day you ever started calling me Salt."

"I look forward to it." Mitch grinned and glanced at Hannah. "You home for the summer too?"

Hannah rolled her eyes. "Always the afterthought. And yes, I am home for the summer, maybe even for good. I'm all graduated, or haven't you heard?"

"Already?" Mitch shook his head. "No way you're old enough to be a college graduate."

"You're just bugged because it makes you feel ancient. What are you now, thirty?"

"Twenty-nine," Mitch returned.

A large smile spread across Hannah's face as she shot her sister a meaningful glance. "Hear that, Court? Looks like Mitch can enter The Meltdown Match too."

He leaned against the wall and folded his arms. "No I can't, and neither can you, if that's what you're here to do. Deadline was yesterday."

Hannah cocked her head and gave him a sultry smile as she moved closer and adjusted the collar of his navy and grey plaid shirt. "I'm sure Mr. Big-Wig City Engineer can find a way to sneak our names in."

"Leave me out of this," Courtney said. "I don't want my name anywhere near those ice vases."

"She's lying," Hannah said. "Ignore her."

"If I *could* get you in?" Mitch said. "What's in it for me?"

"A plate of my mother's to-die-for-cinnamon rolls," Hannah said. "Straight from the oven."

Mitch nodded as if mulling over the offer. "Consider it done." He pushed away from the wall and pointed a finger at Hannah. "But those rolls had better be hot."

"They will be."

He moved to walk away, but Courtney stopped him with a hand on his arm. "If my name ends up on one of those sticks, there's going to be a lot more than cinnamon in those rolls."

"Like what?"

"Like, I don't know, *salt* maybe? You do like it better than cinnamon, right?"

Mitch leaned close, giving her one of his mischievous smiles. "Actually, I like salt better than a lot of things."

With a wink, he was gone, leaving Courtney's heart beating like a flock of geese taking flight. He always had been a flirt and she'd always liked it.

Mitch jogged up the stairs, feeling like his day, and possibly summer, had taken a turn for the better. Courtney was back in town and had handed him a golden opportunity.

He rounded the corner, stepped into a small cubicle, and planted his hands on Alyssa's desk. As the administrative secretary, she had the unlucky responsibility of being in charge of The Meltdown Match and wasn't too happy about it.

"Hey, Lys, I have a few more names to add to the contest."

She continued her typing without a glance at him. "Sorry. Deadline's passed. They'll have to wait until next year."

"But I'll be thirty and can't."

Her stubby fingers stopped typing, like Mitch knew they would. She looked up and studied him through thick, black-framed glasses. "I'm sorry, did you just say *you* want to enter?"

"Sure, why not?"

"Because last week you called The Meltdown Match an embarrassment to Heimel."

Mitch shrugged. "Let's just say I've had a change of heart."

Alyssa pursed her lips as she continued to watch him. Although she only had about five years on him, the way she peered at him made him feel like he was back in elementary school, in trouble with his teacher.

"You said a few names. Who else?"

"Courtney and Hannah Spaulding. I ran into them downstairs."

The wariness in her eyes disappeared, replaced by a slight, knowing smile. "Ah. Everything just got a lot clearer. You do know we have over 100 entries, right? Your chances of getting matched with Courtney aren't that great."

Mitch pushed off the desk and regained his full height. "I was thinking we could increase my odds."

A brown eyebrow lifted. "And how are we going to do that?"

"With salt, obviously."

"To you, maybe."

Mitch smiled, more than a little satisfied with himself. "You should have paid more attention in your chemistry classes. If you had, you'd know that salt lowers the freezing point of water."

Realization dawned in Alyssa's slightly magnified eyes. "Well, aren't you a regular Einstein."

"You mean Pasteur. Einstein was a physicist, not a chemist."

"Whatever." Her expression turned calculating, making Mitch suddenly wary. "I'll help you on one condition."

"What?"

"I need you to take the burger-flipping shift from eleven to two tomorrow."

Mitch hesitated. It would be much less complicated to pick up a phone, ask Courtney out, and avoid the hassle of burger duty and frozen salt water. But there was a reason he'd always kept things at the teasing, just-friends status. Something about her intimidated the heck out of him, and he'd never been able to bring himself to say, *Hey, I like you. Want to go out sometime?*

He'd much rather let the sun take the risk, and if flipping burgers for three hours is what it took to make that happen, so be it.

"Count me in," he said.

Two

—⊚⊚⊚⊚—

The clock on Courtney's nightstand registered 4:20 AM. She blinked sleepy eyes at it as sunlight filtered its way around the outer corners of her blackout blinds, daring her to go back to sleep and miss the dawning of a wonderful, unique day. Today, the sun would shine down from its highest annual altitude, creating the longest day of the year. For those in Heimel, sunset wouldn't come until close to midnight.

Courtney's arms stretched high over head as a small smile touched her lips. She rolled out of bed and opened her blinds, allowing the sun to wash over her face for a few moments. Then she reached for her laptop and plopped down on her bed, tucking a few pillows behind her back. The air felt charged with creativity, as if inspiration waited for the perfect moment to strike.

She stared at the blank computer screen, her mind whirring with possibilities for a new story. What about something set at a dilapidated castle surrounded by enchanted woods? Ireland, maybe? Hannah had always said Courtney should go for an international setting.

Then again, that sounded too much like a fairytale.

What about a story involving The Great Wall of China, or those mystical islands off the coast of Vietnam?

Courtney's fingers fluttered against the keys, not hard enough to make letters appear on the screen. Her expression brightened. What about New Zealand? She could write about a filmmaker who goes there to shoot a documentary about snow skiing then meets a mysterious woman who can control the weather.

She bit her lower lip. That could work—cool setting, lots of potential for intrigue and romance. Yes, that could definitely work.

For the next three hours, Courtney thought, typed, deleted, typed some more, and deleted some more. Something was wrong. Off. The story refused to come together the way her stories usually did. Was it the setting? The plot? The characters? All of the above?

Ugh. She frowned at the sun outside. So much for inspiration.

When the smell of bacon wafted into her room, she highlighted the remaining text, clicked delete, shoved her feet into her slippers, and headed downstairs with an attitude much less optimistic than it had been a few hours earlier.

"Hey, Mom, something smells good."

Dressed in a rose-colored floral apron, with matching curlers in her hair, her mother poured pancake batter onto a skillet. "You're up early. I figured you'd sleep in today and I'd have to keep your breakfast warm."

Courtney moved to the stove and stirred the homemade syrup that simmered there. "I think it's going to take a few days for my body and mind to acclimate to the early sunrise. I've been up since 4:30."

"Good grief, what have you been doing?"

"Writing," Courtney said. "At least trying to. I woke up feeling inspired, only to come up with a whole lot of nothing."

"Sorry to hear it." Her mother flipped over a pancake. "Maybe getting out will help. You and Hannah are going to the June Solstice Days aren't you? That might trigger something."

Courtney turned off the stove and moved the pan to the counter. She dipped her pinky in the syrup and licked the sweet liquid from her finger. "Let's hope so. I promised my agent I'd have a rough draft ready by the end of the summer."

Her mother smiled and patted her cheek. "And you will; I'm sure of it."

Courtney returned the smile, feeling slightly encouraged. Her mother was right. She was in Heimel, after all, and sooner or later, something solid would come to her. It always did. She just hoped it would happen sooner than later.

Courtney eyed the dozens of cylindrical ice vases that lined the tops of several tables—probably about one hundred in all, and not much to look at shape-wise. But the way the light sparkled off the glossy surfaces made for an impressive sight. In this central, roped-off section of the fair grounds, throngs of people milled about, watching and waiting, as if staring at the vases would somehow make them melt faster. Courtney, on the other hand, knew the vases still had hours to go and cared more about whether or not her name appeared on one of the many sticks poking out the top.

She sighed, knowing Mitch had probably made sure her name was there, intermixed with all the others. Or worse—

Salt Spaulding, which was something he'd likely write since he liked to annoy her. Regardless, if The Meltdown Match came to an end and her name wasn't announced, she wouldn't look at the remaining sticks. She preferred to believe that if hers didn't fall first, it didn't exist.

"Look!" A little girl beamed as she pointed. "That vase is almost melted!"

Courtney took a few steps to the side and looked where the little girl pointed. Sure enough, in the men's section, a vase definitely appeared smaller and thinner than those surrounding it.

"Hey, that one seems to be melting faster, too," a woman said, pointing to another vase, this time in the women's section.

Courtney's heartbeat quickened when she saw the stick in the second vase already leaning precariously to the side, waiting for another inch of the ice to liquefy. Unable to pry her eyes away, Courtney continued to watch, feeling like a miracle was happening right before her eyes. Was it coincidence, or was the sun really working its magic, bringing two unsuspecting hearts together? She didn't dare hope one of the names was hers.

Before she caved to the temptation to duck under the ropes and be disappointed, Courtney turned and weaved her way through the throng in search of Hannah. Her eyes scanned the crowed until they settled on a tall, curly-haired guy flipping burgers. Without meaning to, she started forward, forgetting all about the taco salad she and Hannah had agreed on later for lunch. A greasy hamburger suddenly sounded much better.

Courtney paid a few dollars for a plate with chips, potato salad, and a hamburger bun, then made her way to Mitch.

"Hey, aren't you the city engineer?" she said.

He looked up and grinned. "You obviously have me confused with someone else. In case you couldn't tell, I'm a master chef with mad hamburger-flipping skills. Check this out." He scooped up a patty, tossed it in the air, watched as it flipped a couple of times, and caught it with his spatula. His grin widened. "See? No mere city engineer could do that."

Courtney laughed. "You're right. You couldn't be Mitch. No one in their right mind would ever let him near a grill." She leaned closer and lowered her voice. "Back in high school, someone made the mistake of putting him in charge of the hamburgers at a summer party, and he—well, let's just say he gave 'well done' a whole new meaning." Courtney stood on tiptoe and leaned forward to see over the top of the grill. "Those aren't burnt, are they?"

"Very funny." Mitch lowered the lid to block her view and raised an eyebrow in challenge. "Has anyone ever told you that your hair is the color of salt?"

Courtney barely refrained from rolling her eyes. "It's blonde, not white. And no, not many people get that mixed up. Only you and that other guy who burns things."

"Maybe I should leave your burger on a little longer. You know, for old time's sake."

"And maybe I should enter your name in the karaoke contest—you know, for old time's sake," Courtney said, reminding him of the time she'd done exactly that.

Mitch laughed. "Only if you're planning to pass around ear plugs."

"Oh, you weren't that bad." She held up her plate. "One hamburger, please. I need to hurry and eat this before Hannah yells at me for having lunch without her."

He nodded toward the table next to him. "Take a seat. It'll be ready in a sec."

Courtney walked around the grill and sat on the table, letting her legs swing beneath her as she admired how good Mitch looked in jeans and a snug-fitting T-shirt. He filled his clothes out perfectly—not too much and not too little. Mitch had never been into gyms. He preferred to work hard and play harder, and his well-defined, but not excessive, muscles were a result of those labors. When he glanced to the side and caught her staring, she averted her gaze and cleared her throat.

"How did you get roped into doing this, anyway?" she said.

"Haven't you heard? I'm a saint."

Courtney opened her bag of chips and pulled one out, then held the bag out to Mitch. "Alyssa put you up to it, didn't she?"

"Maybe." Mitch grinned as he stole a chip. "But I agreed to it, so that has to count for something."

Courtney smiled, something she did often around Mitch. Moments later, he slipped an unburned patty on her bun with an exaggerated flourish, and she smiled again. Instead of taking her plate to the designated eating area, she stayed put, preferring to eat her lunch next to Mitch.

"Well?" she said.

"Well what?"

"I'm waiting."

"For what?"

"I've been gone for nine months. What have I missed?"

While he cooked and slapped burgers on peoples' plates, Mitch entertained her with story after story of humorous things that had happened around town during her absence. She listened, loving the sound of his voice and the way he could make any situation comical and interesting.

Something about Mitch had always drawn her in. His

good looks, definitely, but Courtney had dated plenty of handsome guys. It was more than that. The way he teased her. The way he looked at her and smiled just that way—as if he'd reserved the real him for her alone. Courtney always had to catch herself from doing something stupid like fall for him or write that face into one of her stories. Mitch could have his pick of anyone, and although he made jokes about salt being his favorite, his actions proved that his tastes ran more toward cinnamon and allspice.

Besides that, come the end of the summer, Courtney would be leaving again—which was exactly what she should do right now. Get away before she let herself fall under his spell even more.

She brushed the crumbs from her fingers and hopped off the table, but as she opened her mouth to say she'd see him later, a voice crackled over the loudspeaker.

"The Meltdown Match has officially ended. If you would please make your way to the middle of the fairgrounds, the winners will be announced."

Three

———⊚⊚⊚———

F eeling suddenly conspicuous, Mitch avoided Courtney's gaze. The results of The Meltdown Match were usually announced later in the day, typically around four or five. Not—he glanced at his watch—one. He'd told Alyssa not to add too much salt, but would she listen to him? No. And now, not only did two vases melt way faster than the rest, but the city engineer just happened to be one of the winners.

That didn't look suspect at all.

"Wow, that was fast," Courtney murmured.

Mitch sneaked a glance and found her staring toward the middle of town with a faraway look in her eyes, probably wondering who'd manipulated the contest. He ducked his head and concentrated on flipping a burger that didn't need to be flipped.

"You did listen to me, right?" she finally said. "You left my name out of it?"

"Yeah. Of course."

"Good." Her voice sounded hesitant, as if she didn't believe him. "So . . . you coming?"

He shook his head, grateful for an excuse to stay. "Can't. My shift doesn't end for another hour."

"Oh." She threw her plate into a nearby trashcan. "Well, thanks again for the burger and company. It was . . . really good."

Was she talking about the burger or his company?

Mitch bit his lip as he watched her go, wondering what she'd think when she saw how fast their vases had melted compared to the others. Would she be happy? Disappointed? Would she suspect him? With a roll of his eyes, he returned his attention to the grill. He should have stayed out of it and let the sun decide their fates. Or better yet, he should have manned up, left both of their names out, and just asked her out.

Courtney lay on her bed, staring dreamily at her bedroom ceiling. She'd won. She'd actually won the contest. And not only that, but Mitch—the man she'd been half in love with for as long as she could remember—had been chosen as her match. Her heart beat wildly at the thought, like it had all afternoon, ever since the results had been announced. She'd tried to talk her heart down, but it was no use. No matter how many times she told herself it was only a coincidence, that the sun really didn't moonlight as a matchmaker, her heart wouldn't listen. It didn't want to listen. It wanted to believe in magic.

If she and Mitch were meant to be, then maybe she could finally stay put in Heimel and her writing wouldn't suffer as a result. The universe had promised a lifetime of happiness, right?

An almost giddy sensation started in her stomach and spread throughout her body. She couldn't help but feel like she'd been granted her most-desired wish. On the nightstand, her cell chimed with a text. She picked it up and smiled when Mitch's name appeared.

Looks like were MFEO. Maybe that's why I like salt so much.

Courtney's smile widened, for once not bugged by the nickname. *You lied,* she wrote back.

His response came moments later. *I wanted those cinnamon rolls. So . . . pick you up at four? Too early?*

Too late, more like. But he probably had to work so Courtney would take what she could get. At least he hadn't said six or seven.

Four it is.

Four

ourtney drifted to sleep, dreaming of a beautiful, outdoor solstice wedding, in full view of the big, bright, blessed sun. Wildflower garlands lined the aisle, and Mitch had never looked so handsome standing beside her in a black tux. When they were pronounced man and wife, he took her in his arms and lowered his mouth to hers. The long-awaited moment was finally happening.

But his lips had barely brushed against hers when a drummer in the band began banging on his drums, ruining the moment. Courtney frowned and looked around, trying to spy the culprit. Why would someone do that during the middle of her wedding?

The banging came again, this time louder.

Her eyes blinked open slowly, and the beautiful scene vanished, along with her smile. The banging continued, only it wasn't the drums, it was something else. A knocking—on her window.

Groggily, she rolled from bed and stumbled forward then pulled her heavy curtains aside. A familiar dark shadow stood directly in front of her. She gasped and jumped, letting the curtain fall back. What was Mitch doing here? Heart pounding, she moved the curtain aside again, throwing it over her shoulder so she could open the window. Chilly, early morning air blew in as she stared at him in confusion.

"What are you doing?"

He wore an orange hoodie and a lopsided smile. "Picking you up for our date."

"But you said four."

"Right." Mitch pointed over her shoulder at the clock on her nightstand. The digital numbers glowed 4:05.

She spun back toward him. "You meant four in the *morning*? Who plans a date for that early?"

He shrugged, looking sheepish. "Sorry. Guess I should've clarified. I thought you'd understand, since this is a solstice date, and the sun rises a little after four."

Courtney blinked through the dim early morning light, her thoughts frantic. Watching the sun rise with Mitch sounded perfectly romantic, but . . . her hand flew to her hair at the same time she looked down, taking in her oversized T-shirt and flannel pajama bottoms.

When her eyes met Mitch's again, his lopsided smile returned. "You look cute," he said. "Just put on some shoes, grab a jacket, and meet me outside. You can come back later to change. Hurry, though, or we'll miss it."

Courtney let the curtain fall and raced to her bathroom where she ran a brush through her hair at the same time she brushed her teeth. She tugged on socks, strapped on a bra, shoved her feet into sneakers, grabbed a jacket, and ran outside, where she found Mitch on her front porch, leaning against a post, looking handsome and put-together in the early morning light. She suddenly wished she'd taken another minute or two to throw on some jeans.

"About time." He reached for her hand and tugged her toward his dusty-blue Jeep. "I'm blaming you if we miss it."

"Two letters, Mitch. Two. *A.M.* Seriously, how hard would have that been to add those to your text?"

Mitch chuckled. "Give me some credit. Why would I wait until the afternoon when I could pick you up in the morning?"

She let the nickname slide. "Because that's when normal people start their dates?"

Mitch opened her door and paused, looking into her eyes. "I think right now is better." The way he said it, without a hint of sarcasm, made Courtney feel like he meant it. Warmth spread through her body, forcing away the chill. She almost forgot to breathe as she climbed into his Jeep.

Mitch drove toward the other end of town and down a winding road toward the lake before pulling to a stop in front of a beautiful rambler that looked more like a ski chalet than a cabin. Not too small and not too big, the combined stone and wood architecture made a picturesque sight nestled between pines and aspens.

"Where are we?" Courtney asked as he led her up the steps and along the wrap-around porch.

"My house."

She stumbled, tightening her hold on his hand to keep from falling. Did he just say this was his house? "But I've never even seen this place."

"It didn't exist until I built it." Mitch stopped by a wooden table on the back patio and gestured for her to sit down. "I moved in a few weeks ago."

"You built this?" Courtney walked toward the window and peered through it. Thanks to a light inside, she could make out knotty wood cabinets, granite counters, and a massive stone fireplace. For a second, she caught a glimpse of herself curled up on the leather sofa with her laptop. Slowly, she turned around to face the lake, trees, and mountains in the distance.

"Wow. It's uh . . ." How could she possibly describe the awe she felt? There were no words. "You really built this?"

Mitch sat down and pulled out the chair next to him, gesturing again for her to sit down. "Most of it. It took a few years, but my dad and brothers helped a ton, so I've got some major sweat equity to repay. I've always loved this property."

Courtney somehow found her way into the seat. "I . . . had no idea. It's amazing. You're amazing. I don't know what else to say. I'm in awe."

"Glad you like it."

"Like it? I love it." She gestured over her shoulder. "I'm so going to borrow that sofa when I start working on my next book. The view is incredible."

"You're welcome to it whenever you want." He reached across the table for a carton of juice and filled two plastic cups before pulling a package of doughnuts from a bag. "Orange, pineapple, and strawberry juice and old-fashioned doughnuts—your favorites, right?"

Courtney's breath caught in her throat as she stared at the table, feeling like she'd been dropped into an alternate reality. An amazing alternate reality. "How did you know?"

"You always ate them after our group hikes way back when. It was kind of hard to miss. All the other girls brought bananas or apples."

He was right. Old-fashioned doughnuts were one of Courtney's guilty pleasures—something she'd always brought along to help combat the jealousy from watching him hold another girl's hand or put his arm around another girl's shoulder. Mitch never failed to invite his current girlfriend along on their group outings.

But now, here she was, on her own date with Mitch Winters.

"Look, here it comes." Mitch pointed at the horizon. "Try telling me that isn't a view worth waking up for."

The sun emerged over the horizon, casting a shimmering glow over everything it touched. As Courtney watched, something awakened inside her, breathing new life into her soul and making her feel a connection with everything around her. She felt so peaceful, so full of an indescribable feeling that made her want to stay right here, with Mitch, forever. The sun was working its magic.

"It's beautiful," she murmured. Could Mitch feel it too? She sneaked a glance at him and immediately wished she hadn't. He looked happy and content, but that was about it. Her heart deflated.

She squinted at the sun, willing the wonderful feeling back. "Do you still hunt?"

"Every now and then, but I'm more into fishing these days. A couple of times a year, I head down to Kenai for a week, charter a boat, and stock up. I've become pretty good friends with the guy who owns the boat, so he always takes me to the best places."

"That's great."

"Just wait until tonight. I have some salmon marinating in the fridge for dinner. I know how much you like salmon." He seemed to know a lot of things.

"I do, although it's been a while since I've had it. You'd think, living near the coast in California, I would have eaten more seafood, but it doesn't taste as good as it does here."

Mitch polished off the last of his doughnut and brushed the crumbs from his hands. "Are you planning to head back at the end of the summer?" He said it casually, as if he didn't care either way. It shouldn't have stung, but it did.

"No, I'll try somewhere new. I haven't figured out where yet."

"What do you mean?"

Courtney attempted to smile, but it probably looked as fake as it felt. "It's sort of my thing. I start working on a story in Heimel then move to wherever I decide to set the book. I get to know the area, get a job, meet people, and work on my manuscript. When I finally submit the book, I come back home to start the process all over again. It sounds kind of intense, but it's—"

"Exhausting?"

"I was going to say an adventure."

Mitch leaned back in his chair and tossed his plastic cup in a garbage can. "So basically, you're a commitment-phobic drifter."

"And superstitious," Courtney added.

A smile sprang to his lips, and a teasing glint appeared in his eyes. "Does that mean you really think there's something to this meltdown match thing?"

Courtney's face flushed. "I'm not *that* superstitious," she said quickly, although the words sounded like a lie to her.

Mitch leaned closer, resting his elbow on the table. "You're either superstitious or you're not. Take your pick."

Courtney forced herself to look him straight in the eye. "Not."

He laughed—a deep, almost melodic sound that seemed to echo off the lake and surrounding mountains. She loved hearing him laugh, even if it was at her expense.

She pushed the bag of doughnuts away and changed the subject. "Now that you've gotten me up at an obscene hour, what's on the schedule for the rest of the day? Hopefully a nap?"

"Together?"

"No."

Mitch grinned. "First I'm going to take you home to change, and"—He leaned over and sniffed the air around her—"shower."

She slugged his arm. "Not funny."

"Then it's a day jam-packed full of stuff to remind you why Alaska is the best place on earth to live."

"I already know that."

His eyebrow rose. "All evidence to the contrary, Miss Commitment-Phobic Drifter who's planning to move away by the end of the summer."

"Maybe I'll surprise everyone and decide to stay this time." Thanks to the sun, maybe she really would.

"That's my goal."

Courtney shot him a look, trying to read his expressions. Was this just fun banter to him, or something more? She couldn't tell. "So in only one day, you think you can convince me to stay in Alaska for good?"

He shrugged. "I'll start today, and we'll see how long it takes."

"What if it takes all summer?"

"Then it takes all summer." Mitch pointed at the sun still peeking above the horizon. "According to that large round ball of fire, we're meant to be together. How's that going to work if you up and leave?"

Yet another comment Courtney had no idea how to take. Was he making fun of the legend or did he, like her, want to believe that it really could be? While part of her hoped that he did, another part—the doubting part—worried that by agreeing to this date, she'd set herself up for a whole lot of heartache.

Five

Mitch bit back a smile at Courtney's look of concentration as they floated in his small fishing boat in the middle of the lake. Fishing was supposed to be relaxing, but she appeared rigid and tense, as though everything hinged on whether she could get a fish to take the bait.

"This isn't a competition," Mitch reminded her.

Courtney offered a fake smile and went right back to furrowing her brows as she slowly reeled in her line. "Sorry, this just brings back memories of fishing with my dad. He used to get so frustrated with me because I was always tangling the line or catching the hook on something. It made me never want to—"

She gasped and lurched forward, nearly toppling out of the boat. If Mitch hadn't been quick to grab her arm and pull her back, she probably would have.

"I caught one!" She turned the reel quicker, almost frantic. "I can't believe I actually caught one! This has never happened to me before." Her lips widened into a huge smile.

"I totally get it now—why you like this. It's actually fun when you catch something."

Mitch couldn't help his answering smile. If anything could be counted on in life, it was that Courtney would do or say something to surprise him. She was the most unpredictable person he'd ever met, which was probably what made her such a great writer.

When the fish finally broke the surface—a big, ugly catfish—she dropped her fishing pole and skittered backwards, rocking the boat. Mitch couldn't hold back his laughter. The reel spun like crazy while the fish tried to make its getaway. He grabbed the pole and started bringing the fish back in.

"What was that thing?" Courtney said.

"Congratulations, you just caught one of the vermin of this lake. That was a catfish."

"It had whiskers."

"That's probably why they call it a *cat*-fish."

Courtney shot him a glare before shifting positions. She eyed the line with a nervous expression, squirming a little when the fish resurfaced. "What are you going to do with it?"

"I thought we'd fry it up for dinner instead of the salmon."

"Very funny."

He worked to loosen the hook then tossed the slimy, wriggling fish back in the water before holding out the fishing pole for Courtney to take.

She shook her head, refusing to accept it. "I don't understand what you see in this sport. You could spend all day here and not catch anything—or worse, catch something like that."

"What happened to all the talk about this being fun?"

"Call it temporary insanity."

Mitch laughed again, something he didn't usually do while fishing. Typically, this was his time to get away from life, to think and let nature rejuvenate him. But being here with Courtney made him feel lighter and happier than he'd felt in a long time. He liked having her along.

With a thunk, he set her pole on the floor of the boat and rested his elbows on his knees. "Okay, so I obviously didn't sell you on fishing, but don't give up on it just yet. Maybe you could even think of today as fodder for your next book and write a story about a fisherman who talks to fish or something."

Courtney drew her lower lip into her mouth, as if seriously considering his suggestion. "A fisherman with a sixth sense who happens to know right where to fish every time. That's actually not a bad idea."

Mitch raised an eyebrow. "Really? A guy who can talk to fish?" It sounded pretty lame to him.

"Not talk," Courtney said. "Feel."

He shrugged, still not seeing it. "Let me guess, he'll fall in love with a mermaid."

Courtney shook her head. "I write magical realism, not fantasy. So no. She'll be a journalist or a photographer—someone who's heard stories about a guy that has never had a bad day of fishing. She'll want to investigate."

Mitch still wasn't sure about the idea. "Just promise me you'll throw in some pirates or something."

Her lips twitched. "Like *Swiss Family Robinson*?"

"No, like *Pirates of the Caribbean*."

"I told you. I don't write fantasy."

"What about a shark attack then?" Mitch said. "Or maybe the guy could get swallowed by a whale and have to talk his way out of it. That would be cool."

Courtney laughed. "Remind me to never come to you for plot ideas. They're terrible."

"Hey, who suggested the fisherman idea?"

"As a *joke*." She smiled then leaned over the edge of the boat and ran her fingers through the water, probably working through plot ideas. Mitch took the opportunity to watch her and the way her nose turned up a tiny bit at the end. A breeze whipped her hair behind her, and with the lake and mountains in the background, the picture she made could easily work on a cover of *Outdoor Life*. Only Courtney didn't need heavy makeup. She was a natural beauty.

Mitch wanted to see that smile every day, make her laugh, and listen to whatever it was she had to say. He wanted to run his fingers through her silky hair, hold her close, and taste her lips. He wanted her in his life for longer than a few months out of the year.

But ever since high school, her MO had always been come and go, come and go—something that had a bipolar effect on him. Whenever she showed up, Heimel became vibrant and exciting, like three-dimensional renderings of a construction design. When she left, it flattened back to a dull, lifeless two-dimensional line drawing.

If only he could convince her to stick around.

Courtney looked his way and caught him staring, and Mitch quickly moved to secure the hooks on both fishing poles. Then he started the small engine and steered the boat toward the small dock. It was time to do something else—something he knew she'd like.

Six

Courtney accepted the helmet with a grin and put it on. She climbed on the back of the 4-wheeler, scooted close to Mitch, and wrapped her arms around his muscular waist, resisting the impulse to bury her face in his back and breath in the intoxicating outdoor scent that was all him. Hopefully this would be a long ride.

"You good?" Mitch called as he started the engine.

"Perfect." She held on a little tighter just because she could.

They spent the next several hours climbing trails, racing through meadows and pointing out moose, elk, eagles, and even a bear. Courtney hadn't felt this content in a long time.

When Mitch drove them to a peak that overlooked Heimel and killed the engine, Courtney reluctantly let go of her hold on him and climbed off to admire the spectacular view. The valley stretched out below them in a lush blanket of greens and browns. Birds chirped, and that raw, earthy scent she loved filled her senses.

"Coming?" Mitch said.

Courtney turned around to find him sitting on a blanket, patting the ground next to him. She smiled and sank down beside him, wishing she could snuggle up and rest her head against his shoulder. Instead, she accepted the sandwich he held out.

"Thank you," she said, turning her face toward the sun. "This place really is beautiful."

"You're only now noticing that?"

She smiled. "No, I've always noticed. But there's something different about leaving and coming home. It sort of feels like a dormant part of me suddenly comes alive. I love that feeling."

He shifted positions to look at her. "I don't get it. If you love it so much here, why not move back for good? You can write anywhere."

Courtney took a small bite of her sandwich and munched it slowly. "I need to do research, and I like seeing new places."

When she said nothing more, he shook his head. "Sorry, not buying it. You can always put down roots and still travel to your heart's content."

She let out a breath and bit her lip. Did she dare tell him the real reason? Would he laugh? File it away as something else he could tease her about? Probably.

And yet she wanted him to know, to understand. "Remember how I told you I'm superstitious?"

"Yeah."

"I wasn't joking." She paused, plucking the leaves off a nearby bush. "From the time I was little, I've always known I wanted to be a writer. In high school, I started submitting my work to agents, but they all shot me down. So I stayed here and went to college for a year in Anchorage, took every creative writing class I could, and went to every writing conference anyone offered. Then I applied what I learned and wrote my first magical realism novel. I thought it was great, but still, no bites. Out of desperation, I took the plunge and transferred to NYU the following year, where I wrote another novel, again with no luck."

The bush was beginning to look sparse. Courtney seemed to realize it too because she stopped plucking and began tearing the leaves instead. "Then something amazing happened. I came back here for the summer and felt that feeling I just told you about. It was like my mind woke up. I wrote a rough draft quicker than I'd ever written one, but when I went back to revise, it was like my mind decided to go dormant again. So I transferred my records to Texas—the place where the book was set—and immersed myself in the culture. The fine-tuning came easier there, and I was able to finish my revisions. Then I sent it out and about died when ten agents requested it—five of whom offered to represent me. Two months later, I signed my first publishing contract."

Courtney paused, wondering what was going through Mitch's mind. Did he think she was crazy, or did he understand?

He picked up a rock and chucked it over the ledge the way you'd throw a rock to skip it across a lake. "Let me get this straight," he said. "You come here to be inspired, but when that so-called well of inspiration runs dry, you feel the need to move away so it can be full and running over by the time you come back." Surprisingly enough, his words didn't sound mocking.

She nodded. "I know it sounds crazy, but writing is now my career, and I can't afford for Heimel to stop inspiring me."

Mitch shifted positions, turning around so he could face her head on. He raised his knee and rested one elbow on it as he studied her. "Have you ever considered that maybe your earlier books weren't accepted because you weren't ready? That it wasn't the right story, or you didn't have enough experience yet?"

"Of course," Courtney said. "And I know that has a lot to do with it. But it still doesn't change the fact that I really do feel inspired when I come home—and it's a feeling that doesn't last. Sometimes I sort of feel cursed—like how Davy Jones can only step foot on land once every ten years. Only at least I get a few months out of every year. "

Almost absentmindedly, Mitch began tracing the perimeter of her fingers, up and over each one. Tingles ran up her arm, making Courtney feel like she'd be catapulted back to her beautiful dream from that morning. She clamped her mouth shut and held still, too afraid that if she moved or said the wrong thing, he'd stop.

His fingers finally closed around her hand, and his gaze met hers. "You could always try to stay this time, just to see. You never know, maybe the change of seasons would give you the same renewed feeling." His eyes had taken on an uncharacteristic vulnerability, as if he really did want her to stay, that part of his happiness might even depend on it.

Her heart beat faster as she stared back. What was happening? Was she experiencing the magic of the sun right now? Mitch had never done more than flirt with her, tease her, invite her on group outings or give her giant bear hugs when she returned.

But here—now—with the rays of that beautiful sun streaming down on them, Mitch leaned closer. His hand moved from her fingers to her face, tucking a stray lock of hair behind her hair and sending chills down her spine. Courtney's heart pounded. She willed him to lean closer still, to brush his lips against hers. Her eyes drifted shut, and she felt herself tilting forward as if compelled to do so.

Kiss me.

His hand moved to the back of her neck, but his warm lips didn't cover hers. Instead, they landed on her forehead, giving her a lingering kiss before drawing away. Cool air rushed between them, reminding her of that morning, when her wonderful dream had been rudely interrupted.

Her eyes flickered open to see uncertainty in his expression, possibly even regret. Her face flushed as heavy disappointment settled in her stomach. A forehead kiss was something you'd give a sister, a child in need of comfort, or the girl who'd never be more than a friend.

Courtney knew all about forehead kisses—she'd written plenty of them into her books.

Seven

Salmon juices sizzled on the grill as Mitch watched Courtney from the corner of his eye. Ever since the stupid forehead kiss, things had been awkward between them. He didn't like it. Why hadn't he just given her a real kiss instead of chickening out? At least then he would have known from her response whether she'd wanted it or not. Now he was stuck wondering if she had been disappointed or grateful.

He'd tried to dispel the awkwardness by taking her to the fairgrounds for some flea market browsing, but it had only made things worse. As the couple who'd won The Meltdown Match, one too many knowing smiles came their way, so he'd finally brought her back to his place for dinner. Now she sat on the railing surrounding his back patio, dangling her feet while taking in the views and saying nothing.

Mitch bit his lip, mentally kicking himself yet again for being such a wuss.

Courtney twisted around, swung her legs up and over the railing, and hopped down from her perch. She approached him with slow, hesitant steps, her hands shoved in the back pockets of her skinny jeans. "Are you sure you don't need any help? I feel lame sitting here while you do all the work."

Mitch's arms itched to pull her to him and kiss her long and hard. Maybe then this nervous tension would go away and leave them alone. Maybe then he'd know if she was as crazy about him as he was about her.

He scooped the salmon from the grill, turned the heat off, and lifted the plate. "Everything's ready," he said, setting the plate on the table. He went inside and retrieved a salad from the fridge and twice-baked potatoes from the oven.

When he emerged from the house, Courtney eyed the table. "Wow, this looks amazing. When did you learn to cook so well?"

"You haven't tasted it yet."

"If it tastes as good as it smells, it's going to be fantastic."

Mitch pulled out a chair for her then sat down, racking his mind for something to say— preferably something funny that would make her laugh. When he came up empty, he focused on his food and rebuked himself yet again for botching things so badly earlier. Of all the dates to go wrong, this was the worst. It was too important—*she* was too important.

"I've been thinking more about the fisherman with a sixth sense idea, and I'm liking it more and more," she said.

Mitch wondered if she'd said that to be nice—something that might put an end to the awkward silence—because the fisherman idea *had* been a joke. It stunk.

He played along anyway. "Yeah?"

"It's a good thing I don't have my laptop or notebook with me. I'd probably start jotting down some notes."

He had no idea what to say to that. "I have a notebook inside if you'd like."

"No." She waved his suggestion aside. "I was only joking."

But was she? Mitch changed the subject, and after some painful small talk to get them through dinner, Courtney insisted on doing the dishes. "It's the least I can do after all you've done today," she said, picking up his plate. "Besides, I've wanted to take a peek inside ever since you brought me here, and this is my chance."

Mitch followed with the glasses. "Want a tour?"

"Of course."

Together, they made quick work of cleaning up, and once the last dish had been loaded, Mitch held out his hand, hoping she'd take it. "Ready?"

She hesitated a second, then placed her hand in his. It felt soft and small and perfect, especially when her fingers tightened around his and she returned the pressure of his grip.

He gave her hand a tug and led her down the hall. "The house has four bedrooms, two and a half baths, a den, vaulted ceilings, and a lot of stone and wood. I wanted it to have more of a chalet feel."

Courtney peeked inside each bedroom as they passed. Although they were pretty much empty, with little to no furniture, she seemed to like what she saw. In the master bedroom, she relinquished his hand and took her time looking around. Mitch shuffled his feet as he waited, wondering what she thought. With only a bed and nightstand, there wasn't much to see, but the stone fireplace was cool, along with the wooden beams on the vaulted ceiling.

Courtney finally faced him and cocked her head. "This

room is beautiful, but it's too empty. Take that fireplace, for example. It's gorgeous, but where's the loveseat to curl up on? And these hardwood floors—" Her foot tapped the boards. "Spectacular. But it could really use a rug to cozy it up. And those windows." She gestured toward the floor-to-ceiling windows that spanned the far end of the room. "Talk about an amazing view. You need a comfy recliner right there."

A teasing glint appeared in her eyes as she approached him, resting both hands on his chest and shaking her head in mock disappointment. "I have to say, I'm feeling a little let down. You could really use a woman's touch in here."

With her standing this close, touching him and smelling faintly of citrus, he had to disagree. His room had never felt *less* empty. "Are you volunteering?" he said.

"Give me some time and a decent budget, and you'll wonder how you ever called this place home before."

Mitch covered her hands with his and stared into her beautiful green, almost blue eyes. "I don't know. It's feeling pretty homey right now."

A moment passed when they booth stood there, saying nothing. Mitch's heart rate increased to the point where Courtney could probably feel it pounding beneath her fingers. Now was his chance to do what he should have done before, to pull her to him and find out if her heart was racing as wildly as his.

Confusion appeared in her eyes, and her hands pulled free from his, dropping back to her side. "You said there was a den?" Her voice sounded a little shaky.

Mitch resisted the impulse to curse and nodded toward the doors. "Yeah, that way." Without taking her hand this time, he led her down the hall and to the right, toward a small alcove outside a set of dark, wooden doors. He paused with his hands on the handles, hoping against hope that she'd like what was on the other side. Then he drew in a breath and swung them wide, stepping aside.

Courtney's eyes widened as she walked into the room and turned a slow circle around, taking in everything. Mahogany bookcases spanned one wall, floor-to-ceiling windows covered another, and a chair sat adjacent to a small fireplace opposite the windows, next to a beefy, off-centered desk that angled toward the windows.

Mitch had taken his time with this room.

"Okay, I was so wrong," Courtney breathed. "You don't need a woman's touch, not if you could come up with something like this." She walked to the bookcase and ran her fingers along the spines of several of the books. "This is seriously the most beautiful room I've ever seen."

Her fingers stilled over a spine, and she pulled out a book. She turned to face him, a look of surprise on her face. "You have my books."

Mitch pushed away from the desk and moved toward her, taking the book from her hands. "I like them all, but this is my favorite."

Her eyes snapped to his. "You've read them?"

"Every word. You're an amazing writer."

Courtney sucked in a quick breath and looked at her feet, but not before Mitch caught a glimpse of moisture pooling in her eyes. She half laughed, half snorted. "I can't believe I'm crying." She shook her head. "It's just . . . Well, the fact that you've read them all means . . . a lot to me."

Mitch replaced the book on the shelf before taking her hands in his, drawing her close. "Want to know why I finished this room first?"

She nodded, her eyes searching his.

A pit of nervous anxiety settled in Mitch's stomach. "Because of you."

Silence. Only the widening of her eyes indicated that she'd heard him.

He felt as though he'd just gotten off the ski lift at the top of a steep mountain with nowhere to go but down a steep run. He drew in a deep breath and pushed off. "Courtney, I've always been crazy about you. But when you come back to town, you're never here long, and you're always so busy writing that I don't get to spend much time with you. When I designed this room, I sort of did it with you in mind, thinking that it might entice you to spend some of your writing time over here." He paused, his fingers trembling in hers. "Every time I'm in here, it reminds me of you, and makes me feel like you're not so far away and out of reach."

"Really?" More tears glistened in Courtney's eyes, but this time she didn't blink them away. One slipped out and trailed down her cheek, followed by another.

Mitch's thumb moved to her cheek, wiping the tear away. "Really."

She sniffed and blinked away the tears. "Then why did you kiss me on the forehead earlier? I wanted it to be a real kiss, and when it wasn't, I thought it meant that you didn't care. At least not as much as I did."

Her words worked their way into Mitch's heart, filling and expanding it. Not wanting to waste another second or let this moment pass, he dipped his head and covered her lips with his, showing her exactly how much he did care. Her arms wound around his back and her fingers clung to his shirt as her lips moved against his with increased pressure, searching, seeking, and tasting.

A feeling of exhilaration flowed through Mitch's body, filling him with an amazing energy. It was a kiss unlike any he'd ever known. Nothing had ever felt so good, so right. Courtney belonged here, in his arms—not in New York or California or Texas, but here.

She couldn't leave again. She couldn't.

Courtney finally drew back, looking up with an expression filled with warmth and joy. Mitch smiled as his fingers traced along her jaw line. "If you only knew how long I've wanted to do that."

"If you only knew how long I've waited for you to do that."

He chuckled and leaned in for one more kiss, more lightly this time, then led her out of the den and to the great room, where he closed the blinds, dimmed the lights, and started a fire in the fireplace. They spent the rest of the evening snuggling, talking, and kissing.

When the sun finally approached the horizon close to midnight, Mitch took Courtney outside to the front porch. He stood behind her and wrapped his arms around her shoulders, pulling her close as the sun slowly disappeared behind the mountains, marking an end to one of the longest, and now best, days of the year.

"This is the most perfect ending to any day I've ever had," Courtney whispered.

Mitch couldn't agree more.

Eight

Mouth-watering smells of homemade cinnamon rolls filled Courtney's senses as her eyes blinked open. She stretched her body and smiled at her bedroom ceiling. With dreams of Mitch and a new plot for a book fresh in her mind, it was easy to leave her bed behind and make her way to the kitchen, where her parents and Hannah were already eating breakfast.

Her father eyed her from over the top of his paper. "What time did you get in last night?"

"Around one."

Hannah wiggled her eyebrows. "Was Mitch trying to make a new Guinness record or something, because that had to be the longest June solstice date ever."

Courtney only smiled. She dropped a huge cinnamon roll on her plate and slid her chair next to her mother's. "Thanks for breakfast, Mom."

"You look happy this morning," her mother commented.

A giddy feeling zipped through Courtney's body as she pulled apart the roll and popped a piece into her mouth. Morning had never been so cheery and bright, and cinnamon rolls had never tasted so good. "Probably because I am happy."

Hannah and her mother gave each other knowing smiles, and Hannah started chanting, "Courtney and Mitch, sitting in a tree, K-I-S-S-I-N-G—"

"We were in his house, not a tree," Courtney corrected.

Hannah burst out laughing while her father lowered his paper once more, giving Courtney a you've-got-some-explaining-to-do look.

"You went out with Mitch Winters?" A man of few words, he'd always been a little behind when it came to keeping up with his daughters' social agendas.

"We won The Meltdown Match."

Her father harrumphed as her mother asked, "So . . . you and Mitch . . ."

"Will be spending a lot more time together," Courtney finished. "In fact, I'm heading to his house this morning to get some writing done. Since he's got to work, it will be quiet there, and wow, you should see his new place. It's gorgeous."

Her mother nodded, lips twitching. "I take it you've settled on a plot for your next story, then?"

"I won't know for sure until I get it down on paper, but yeah, I think so."

"Let me guess," Hannah said dryly. "Mitch gave you the idea."

Courtney couldn't help the grin that sprang to her face as she nodded. She felt like a silly, twitterpated teenager who couldn't control her emotions. "Let's just say he's definitely inspiring."

Hannah and her mother exchanged another look, making Hannah giggle. "Somebody's in love," she said in a singsong voice, swirling her juice.

Although Courtney rolled her eyes, a warm feeling spread through her chest, making her wonder if her sister was right. What she felt for Mitch was definitely stronger than anything she'd ever felt before, but was it the always and forever kind of love? The kind she'd written and dreamed about?

It sure felt like it.

An hour later, Courtney knocked on Mitch's front door. When no one answered, she pulled out the spare key he'd given her from her pocket and let herself inside. Her footsteps echoed off the hardwood floor as she made her way to the kitchen, where she put a bag of groceries in the fridge and set a plate of her mom's cinnamon rolls on the counter. Adjusting the strap of her bag with her laptop on her shoulder, she walked to the den. The double doors were already open, the blinds raised, and the chair beckoning. Courtney inhaled the smell of paper and ink, mixed with a hint of Mitch, and smiled. Then she sat down and got to work.

The story came together like no story had before. Scene after scene played out in her mind, and characters became fully formed as her fingers flew over the keys, failing to keep up with her thoughts. Although she'd always been told to write what she knew, Alaska had never seemed that exciting of a place to set a book before. But now, it was perfect.

As the hours passed, her stomach started rumbling. Courtney leaned back in her chair and stretched her arms behind her in satisfaction. Then she rose and went to the kitchen, where she pulled out the bag of groceries and chopped vegetables for gourmet hoagie sandwiches. Mitch had mentioned that he sometimes came home for lunch, and she wanted to have something ready for him if he did.

Soon the rumblings of the garage door sounded, followed by Mitch walking in the door. He tossed his keys on the counter and headed straight to her, taking her in his arms and kissing her soundly enough to make her toes curl. How many times had she dreamed of this happening? Mitch holding her, kissing her, wanting to be with her.

Excited flutters ran through her stomach as she smiled against his lips. "I could really get used to this," she murmured.

"Me too." He drew back and ran his fingers up and down her arms. "Get much done on your story?"

She nodded. "I practically have the whole thing outlined, and I owe it all to you. Not only did you inspire me with the idea, but you gave me the most wonderful place to write it."

"Yeah, well, don't think it doesn't come with strings attached."

"What kind of strings?" She nodded her head toward the counter. "Because I brought you some of my mom's cinnamon rolls *and* made you the best sandwich you will ever taste in your life."

His gaze flicked toward the table and back to her. "That should cover about half."

"Only half?" Her fingers traveled from his waist to his chest to the back of his neck, where they interlocked. She backed him against the counter and pulled his mouth to hers in a kiss that hopefully made up for the other half. When she finally drew back, she felt weak and had to tuck her head against his chest as she struggled to catch her breath.

His arms tightened around her, and he rested his chin against the top of her head. "Wow, Salt," he said. "I'll take one of those anytime."

She poked him in the ribs. "Not if you keep calling me that."

He chuckled. "But it fits so well. I mean, think about it. Salt makes almost everything taste better, the same way you make my life better."

Courtney muffled her laughter in the fabric of his shirt before peeking up at him and shaking her head. "That was the cheesiest thing you've ever said, and my name is Courtney. Say it with me now. Court—ney."

"But it doesn't have the same ring to it." He tried to kiss her again, but she broke free and shook her head.

"Just wait until I come up with an equally fitting nickname for you. You're going to be sorry you ever called me Salt."

He pulled out a barstool, sat down, and reached for one of the hoagies. "I'm quivering with fear."

Nine

Courtney entered the city offices and took the stairs two at a time. Only thirty minutes earlier, she'd officially finished her rough draft, and it was time to celebrate by taking Mitch out for lunch. The book was coming together quicker than any of her others, and although she still had mountains of revision ahead of her, she'd reached a huge milestone and couldn't wait to tell him the news.

Ever since The Meltdown Match, her scattered life and question mark of a future had become a little less scattered and a little more certain. For the first time since she'd left for college, Courtney wasn't afraid to stay in Heimel permanently. In fact, she wanted nothing more than to sink her roots more deeply into the place she'd never really pulled them from. She wanted the life that Mitch had shown her during the past couple of months.

Every day had been as close to perfection as she could have hoped. She'd spent her days writing and the evenings hanging out with Mitch. They did everything together. Fishing, 4-wheeling, biking, hiking, shopping, rappelling, swimming—even hunting, although Courtney wouldn't let him actually shoot anything, so it was more like animal watching. They played games, cooked dinner, hung out with family and friends, and read books together. The added romance had catapulted a good friendship into something truly amazing, and Courtney had never felt more connected to anyone. Which was exactly why she couldn't wait to see him now.

She rounded a corner and smiled when she spied his secretary. "Hey, Alyssa, how are you?"

Alyssa twirled a pen between her fingers as she returned the smile. "Better and better, thanks to you."

"Me?" Courtney asked, unsure as to why she'd been given credit for Alyssa's good day.

"I now have the happiest, most pleasant boss in the world." Her eyes narrowed as she peered at Courtney through her glasses. "Don't you ever dump him, or I might kill you."

Courtney laughed. Only yesterday, Hannah had pretty much told Mitch the same thing. "Why would I dump him? According to the sun, he's my perfect match."

"The sun and a whole lot of salt," Alyssa muttered, returning her attention to the paperwork on her desk.

Courtney's smile faltered as she tried to make sense of Alyssa's words. Did she mean "Salt", as in *her*, or the stuff people sprinkled on French fries? Either way, it didn't make sense. "What does salt have to do with anything?"

Alyssa glanced up. "Didn't Mitch tell you? We added salt to the water to make your vases melt faster."

"Oh." A heavy feeling slammed into her as she strained to keep a semblance of a smile on her face while Alyssa continued talking, saying words like *romantic* and *sweet*.

Courtney was suddenly eight years old again on Christmas Eve—the much anticipated night that she finally got to stay up to see Santa Claus instead of having to go to bed. For years, she'd imagined how magical and life-changing it would be. Would Santa bring some of his elves? Would she get to see Rudolf and his glowing nose? Would he give her a hug, set her favorite toy under the tree, and tell her she'd been a really good girl? She'd thought of him all year long.

Turned out it was none of the above, because Santa wasn't real. Just like The Meltdown Match wasn't real.

Her heart felt as though it had been poked with a pin, and now it slowly deflated, wrinkling like a balloon.

"Courtney, are you okay?" Alyssa's voice sounded through the fog.

Voices approached from somewhere down the hall, and two men appeared—Mitch and someone else.

"Hey, beautiful, what are you doing here?" He put an arm around her and kissed her cheek before making introductions. Courtney was vaguely aware of trying to smile and shake the man's hand before he left, his footsteps sounding loud as they descended the hard, marble stairs.

Courtney tried to talk herself out of her emotions. The Meltdown Match was a silly contest. It didn't mean anything. She and Mitch were meant to be together because they were meant to be together, not because some huge ball of fire decreed it so. No one in their right mind would place any stock in it at all.

No one except her.

Mitch smoothed his hands up and down her arms. "Hey, something wrong?"

Courtney shook her head slowly, trying to clear it.

"I, uh, need to go make some copies." Alyssa was out of her seat and down the hall in seconds.

Unable to put a stop to her overreaction, Courtney

blinked at Mitch, needing to say something. "The Meltdown Match . . . you added salt . . . to the water?"

His face took on a sheepish expression as he nodded. "It gave me the courage to finally ask you out. You're not mad, are you?"

"No." What Courtney felt didn't resemble anger, more like a keen disappointment that she didn't quite understand. She wasn't eight anymore. She was twenty-seven and should know better than to believe in something like The Meltdown Match.

Why, then, did she suddenly find herself questioning everything? Was her relationship with Mitch even real? Had she conjured up intense feelings because she thought the universe had said she should feel this way? And what about Heimel and her well of inspiration? Would that run dry yet again? She'd been so confident about everything only moments before, but now all her assurances had cracked.

More than ever, Courtney hated the nickname of "Salt."

She drew in a deep breath and took a step back. She needed to get away from Mitch, away from everyone. She needed fresh air to breathe and time to figure out what in the heck had just happened.

"I'm sorry, but I've got to go. I just remembered I have to do . . . something."

Mitch moved toward her, then stopped. His expression reflected confusion and concern, but he didn't try to keep her from leaving. "I'll call you when I get off work."

Courtney nodded, then turned and trotted down the stairs. Only this time, instead of her spirits rising with each excited leap up, they plummeted with each step down.

Ten

When Mitch called after work, Courtney didn't answer. When he called again ten minutes later, she rolled to her side and curled into a ball, hugging her pillow as she gripped her phone, still unsure of what to say. Her cell buzzed with a new text.

I'm coming over.

Her fingers reacted quickly. *Now's not a good time.*

A few minutes passed before the phone buzzed again. *We need to talk.*

She stared at the words. Mitch deserved an explanation—he did—but what could she say? Her feelings felt so jumbled and cloudy. *We do, and we will. Later. I need some time.*

What's going on? This is killing me.

Sorry, was all she could write. And she was. Very sorry. But even after spending all afternoon trying to talk herself out of feeling this way, she couldn't keep the doubting questions or worries at bay. There were no threatening tears, no emotional outbursts. Courtney simply felt empty inside, as though part of her soul had up and left.

A knock sounded at her door before it opened, and Hannah's voice echoed through the quiet room. "Hey, you sick or something? You've been in here for hours."

Courtney said nothing, just gripped her pillow and clutched her phone as if it were her last link to sanity. Her bed moved as Hannah sat down. "What's wrong with you?"

"I'm a mess," Courtney mumbled into her pillow.

A pause. "Wanna talk about it?"

"No."

"Fine, I'll go get Mom. No wait—make that Dad."

Courtney twisted around and glared at her sister. "Don't you dare."

"Me or him—take your pick." Hannah shifted, making herself comfortable. "But since I already know you're messed up, I'm probably the lesser of the two evils, so I'd choose me if I were you."

Courtney sighed and pulled herself up, hugging her knees to her chest. Maybe talking it through with someone would help, and Hannah was the preferred choice. "I just found out that Mitch made our vases out of salt water so they'd melt faster."

Hannah's eyes widened at the same time her smile did. "Are you serious? That's awesome!"

"No," Courtney said. "Not awesome. All this time I've been thinking that we were, you know . . . destined to be together or whatever, and now it turns out we're like every other couple out there who met randomly and happened to make a connection."

The smile faded from Hannah's face, replaced with a look of disbelief. "You can't be serious. Court—hello! You make love sound like an everyday occurrence, when you, of all people, should know better. You've dated and walked away from a lot of guys in the past, but now you're finally with Mitch—a guy you've always liked—and you've never been happier. Don't you dare walk away from him just because you weren't really matched up by the sun." She paused. "I can't believe I had to say that. Now you're making *me* sound crazy."

Courtney sighed. "Believe it or not, I know all that—I do. I just can't make my illogical feelings see logic, if that makes sense. It's like with my writing and Heimel. I could never stay here permanently because this town would become the place I live, not the place that inspires me. Then The Meltdown Match and Mitch happened, and I finally thought that everything had changed. But now I don't know anything anymore."

Hannah's mouth parted as she blinked at her sister. "Oh my heck. You're like one of those athletes who won't cut their hair or wash their socks the entire season because they think it will jinx them."

Courtney brought her knees to her chest and frowned out the window. "Told you I was a mess."

"I'll say." Hannah shook her head in disbelief. "Know what? I think this is one of those times when your over-active imagination is getting the best of you. You live in the real world. You know that, right? A world where apple trees don't grow fruit during the winter, the wind doesn't have healing properties, and the sun's definitely *not* a matchmaker."

Courtney frowned. She'd always liked to believe that her books had the power to inspire, but maybe they didn't. Maybe they only created daydreamers with unrealistic expectations. Like her. So much for thinking this talk would help. It had only made things worse.

"I know," she finally muttered.

"Do you? Really? Because I'm not so sure." Hannah rose

to her feet and walked toward a small bookcase where she pulled out a copy of each of Courtney's four published books.

She held one up. "Remember what inspired this one? You came home for the summer, and Mitch organized a camping trip. It was windy, and I sprained my ankle, but no one had an ace bandage in their first aid kit, so Mitch made a joke about how if wind could heal, it would be better in no time. The next day, you started writing this book."

She tossed it on the bed and held up another. "Remember when you took a semester off and came home in the dead of winter? It was below freezing outside, and to help pass the time, Mitch invited everyone over to his house for games. You said you were craving an apple, and he said not to worry. He had a tree out back that grew apples all year long. Then he disappeared and came back with an apple."

Another book landed by the first before Hannah held up the next. "And this one, about a small town that produces amazing artists? That story came after Mitch made us all drive to Anchorage to see Lilly's painting at that gallery. While we were there, he said that Heimel must have something special in the water, because not only did Lily's painting make it in a gallery, but you'd just published your first book."

The book landed on top of the others as Hannah held up the last one. "What about the time we went spelunking? Don't you remember?"

Hannah's voice seemed to fade into the background as Courtney's gaze dropped to her hands. She did remember now. Everything. The apple. The healing wind. The magical town. And the cave of truth, where no one could lie.

All this time, she'd been giving Heimel credit for her inspiration when it had really been Mitch—the same person who'd inspired her with her latest idea. How had she been so blind? So stupid? So wrong?

Tears sprang to her eyes at the same time Hannah's hand came to rest on her knee, bringing Courtney back to the present. "Don't you see? What you have with Mitch is way more miraculous than winning some stupid ice-melt contest. What you have with him is something some people look for their entire lives and never find."

It was true. Even with tears marring her vision, Courtney could see more clearly now than ever before. A warm feeling spread through her body, taking away the heaviness and weaving in peace and joy. Her sister was right. What she and Mitch had went way beyond superstitions and magic and fantasy.

What she and Mitch had was real.

Her arms went around her sister as she simultaneously laughed and cried. "Thank you so much for pointing out how stupid I am." She sniffed and wiped at her eyes. "You really are the best."

"Duh."

Eleven

Mitch sat in his boat in the middle of the lake and flung his fishing pole forward, casting his line as far as he could. Then he reeled it in, too fast to actually catch anything. Not that he wanted to. What he wanted was for the unsettled feeling in his gut to go away and for the image of Courtney backing away from him to leave his mind.

Normally after a bad day, fishing had a calming effect on him, but today was different. Today he'd lived with the worry that Courtney could walk out of his life yet again. That she'd show up at any moment with the news that it was time for her to move on.

His stomach in knots, Mitch cast the line again before turning the reel as fast as he could, as if retrieving the hook would somehow bring her back. But when the hook resurfaced empty, all it did was serve as a reminder of how he felt. Empty.

Over and over, he cast and reeled, cast and reeled, looking for a solace he couldn't find. She needed some time.

She needed space. She needed distance. From him.

The sick feeling returned with a vengeance, and Mitch threw his fishing pole to the bottom of the boat. It was no use. Not even fishing helped.

"Mitch!" The faraway voice seemed to echo off the lake and surrounding trees.

He looked around, finally spotting long, blonde hair blowing in the breeze and two arms waving at him. Courtney was here. Ready to talk? About what? Mitch still had no clue what had gone wrong. Queasiness filled his stomach as he started the engine and headed for the dock. He pulled up moments later, avoiding her gaze, too afraid of what he'd see.

"Hey." She sounded happy and light. Possibly even bipolar.

Mitch felt more confused than ever. He tied up his boat slowly before stepping onto the dock and eyeing her warily.

She started to move toward him, but stopped and clasped her fingers together, looking suddenly nervous. "I guess you probably want an explanation."

"That all depends on what your explanation is," he said, shoving his hands into the pockets of his khaki shorts.

Courtney took a tentative step toward him and drew in a deep breath. "Okay, so here goes. When I found out that you were behind the contest, I sort of freaked out about, well, everything. I wanted to believe the contest was real, that we really were destined to be together, and then I found out it wasn't. It threw me a little."

Mitch wanted to pull her to him, give her a good shake and tell her that they *were* destined to be together. It was something he'd known for years. But his hands remained at his side and his mouth shut.

"But then Hannah bluntly pointed out that I've been wrong about everything. Especially you."

Him? Courtney had been wrong about him? What was that supposed to mean?

"I don't understand," Mitch finally said.

She approached him and took his hands in hers. "*You're* my inspiration. Not Heimel. Not coming home. You."

For the first time since Courtney had walked out on him earlier, Mitch felt his chest lighten. He had no idea how she'd come to that conclusion, but if it meant she wasn't going anywhere, he'd take it. Or did she mean that?

"Wait, what does that mean, exactly?" Mitch said. "Do you still feel the need to move away and come home to me instead of Heimel? Like I'm some . . . I really don't know what to compare it to. All I know is that I wouldn't be okay with it."

Her lips drew into a smile. "What I'm saying is that I'm here to stay. For good."

"But what about the whole needing to be re-inspired thing?" Mitch wasn't quite ready to believe her. His world had been shaken and it didn't feel right yet.

Courtney intertwined her fingers with his and swallowed. "Look, I don't know what the future holds for me, for us, or for my writing. But what I do know is that from here on out, I'm choosing to believe in us rather than some silly superstitions. I'm in love with you, Mitchell Winters, and I want to be here with you. For always and no matter what."

A light breeze blew past, making him wonder if the wind really did have restorative properties. As it came and went, all of the heaviness and worry and heartache seemed to leave with it. He lifted Courtney's hands, bringing her closer. "You'll really be happy living here with me?"

"Yes," she said without hesitation. "Although I do still want to travel and research places for my books. But I'm hoping you'll come with me."

The corners of his mouth tugged into a smile. "So long

as you don't mind if I check out the engineering side of things while we're there."

"Of course not." A teasing glint appeared in her eyes. "In fact, maybe my next book will be about an engineer."

"Yeah?"

"Yeah."

"Will his name be Mitch?"

"Definitely."

"Will he have x-ray vision and be able to see through roads so people know exactly where to dig?"

Courtney's lips twitched as she shook her head. "No."

"Will he be a brilliant mathematician who never has to use a calculator?"

"No."

"Oh." He shrugged, out of ideas. "I guess he'll have to be the guy who can sense when two people are supposed to be together and manipulates the situation so they are." He grinned as he tugged on a lock of her hair. "Like with salt."

Her forehead creased in thought, and she drew her lower lip into her mouth for a moment before letting it out. "You mean like Cupid?"

Mitch frowned, picturing a naked cherub with a pink bow and tiny white wings. "No, not like Cupid. That was just a joke—a bad one."

"Well, I like it. And considering how all of my ideas have been inspired by one of your bad jokes, it's got merit."

If that was the case, Mitch really needed to stop joking, especially when it came to characters named Mitch. "What about Hercules instead? He's pretty cool."

"No, I like Cupid."

"Zeus? Poseidon? I'd even take Hades."

Her fingers threaded through the hair at the nape of his neck. "I think I've finally figured out the perfect nickname for yours truly—one that will be as fitting and endearing to you as Salt is to me." She grinned. "Cupid."

This conversation was getting out of control. "I don't think so."

"I do." Her fingers pressed on the back of his neck, trying to pull his head toward hers, but Mitch resisted. "Oh, c'mon, Cupid," she said with a slight pout on her lips. "Don't you want to kiss me?"

Mitch grasped for something—anything—to make the nickname go away. "Okay, fine, you win. I promise to stop calling you Salt if you *never* say that word again."

"Cupid, Cupid, Cupid, Cupid, Cupid, Cupid—"

Mitch's mouth covered hers with a kiss meant to erase all thoughts about engineers and books and Cupid. However, as her lips moved across his and her fingers worked their way through his hair, he was the one who forgot about everything but her.

Epilogue

T he day of June Solstice dawned overcast and rainy. Through her window, Courtney frowned at the skies as she smoothed her fingers against the soft satin of her wedding gown. This was all wrong. According to the weather report, the skies were supposed to be clear, the day sunny. A perfect day for an outdoor wedding.

Her mother kept promising that it would clear up, that Courtney needed to finish getting ready, but the clouds didn't break, and the rain continued to splatter lightly against her window pane.

Not good.

Courtney's stomach twisted into knots at the implication. She forced herself to take a deep, calming breath. This was not the universe telling her that she shouldn't marry Mitch or pick another wedding day. It was an unlucky coincidence. That's all.

Horribly unlucky.

Her phone rang with Mitch's ringtone, and Courtney quickly brought it to her ear. More than ever, she needed to hear his voice.

"No, this is not a bad omen, and yes we're still supposed to get married today," Mitch said without preamble. "In fact, this is actually a good sign. It means our married life together will be full of surprises and never dull."

Courtney couldn't help her answering smile. She loved that he knew where her crazy thoughts were headed—and that he still wanted to marry her in spite of them. More than that, he knew exactly what to say to erase the worried lines from her forehead.

"I was just thinking the exact same thing," she said.

"Liar."

Her smile widened. "Okay, Mr. Know-it-all, where are we going to have the wedding now?"

"Outside, near the lake, as planned. It's already set up, and the food is under that gazebo thing you rented, so we're good."

"So long as the food stays dry," she said dryly.

"Exactly."

Courtney rolled her eyes and looked down, picturing rain splattering all over her dress while her short train skidded across the muddy ground. What would her hair look like after a few minutes in this weather? Not like it did now, that was for sure.

"But what about my dress?"

"I don't see a problem. It's not like you're planning to wear it again." A pause. "Right?"

"Well no, but—" It was beautiful and white and expensive, and Courtney didn't want it to get muddy. She wanted it to look clean and perfect for the day her future daughter tried it on. Did she really have to explain that?

"But what?"

Courtney sighed. "My hair will go limp and the pictures will look awful."

"Oh please. You couldn't look awful if you tried, and the pictures will give us a great story to tell our kids one day."

An almost hysterical laugh escaped Courtney's mouth, mostly because she actually found herself considering his suggestion. She threw up her free hand and plopped down on her bed. "Okay fine, Mr. Cupid Man, let's get married in the rain."

"That's my girl. See you in an hour." At least he'd let the Cupid comment slide.

The phone went dead before Courtney could tell him she was only half serious. She frowned out the window once more before turning toward Hannah and her mother. "Looks like the outdoor wedding is still on."

"Sweet!" Hannah said at the same time her mother excused herself to make a few phone calls to track down some umbrellas.

An hour later, Courtney found herself sitting in her dad's car as he pulled into the mess of the designated parking area. She'd exchanged her satin heels for tennis shoes and stepped into the squishy mud, holding her dress high while her mother positioned a large, multi-colored beach umbrella over their heads.

They squished their way to a large tent, where Courtney made her final preparations. Her mother cleaned off her shoes with wet wipes while Hannah fiddled with her hair. Thankfully, someone had brought a clear, plastic umbrella for Courtney's father to carry down the aisle so they could dispense with the brightly colored one.

In no time at all, her mother disappeared, the music started, and Hannah left the tent, carrying a bouquet of fresh wildflowers.

Courtney's dad held out his arm for his daughter. "Ready to go, sweet pea?"

"As ready as I'll ever be." Her feet landed once more in the mud, and Courtney tried not to cringe as they made their way to the back of the crowd, where a live band huddled under a canopy and guests waited with various colored umbrellas. At least the wildflower garland looked lovely and hydrated.

Through the drizzle and beneath her veil, Courtney's eyes met Mitch's. He stood at the front, looking beyond handsome wearing a black tux and holding a matching clear plastic umbrella. Her breath caught in her throat as all thoughts of rain and mud and limp hair faded. In a matter of minutes, she would be his, and he, hers. They would leave this scene as man and wife and spend the rest of their lives together.

It really did feel like a miracle.

She was led to Mitch's side, where she relinquished her father's arm and kissed his cheek. Then she placed her fingers on Mitch's warm palm and smiled when he held out his umbrella so she wouldn't get wet.

"You look beautiful," he mouthed, drawing her close. "You ready for this?"

"More than ready."

"Me, too." He tucked her arm in his and turned to face the pastor. In what seemed like minutes, they were pronounced man and wife beneath a dense canopy of clouds. Although the sun remained hidden, the warmth that spread through Courtney's body made it feel as though it was a clear, sunny day.

Mitch handed the umbrella to the pastor, and raindrops dotted Courtney's face and arms. But it didn't matter, not when his hands framed her face and he looked at her in just that way, as if she were his everything. Courtney raised her mouth to his, smiling when his lips moved gently over hers in a kiss that would be forever engrained in her memory. He kissed her as though she were fragile and precious— something to treasure. Her heart swelled with the kind of love she'd only ever imagined in her mind and written in her books.

In that moment, Courtney's world aligned, as if she'd finally been able to bridge the gap between fiction and real life. She'd always been a wisher, a hoper, a believer in something greater than the ordinary, but today it was no longer wishful thinking. It was reality. Her very own real life fairytale come true.

She couldn't wait to live it all out.

Author's Note

Dear Reader,

Thanks so much for reading! I hope this story took you out of reality for awhile and into a world of escape and rejuvenation because everyone deserves that once in a while.

If you're willing, I'd love a review from you on Goodreads or Amazon or wherever else you'd care to post one. And if you'd like to be notified of future new releases, you can sign up for my newsletter list or check out more of my books on RachaelReneeAnderson.com.

Thanks again, and happy reading!

Rachael

About Rachael Anderson

Rachael Anderson is a *USA Today* bestselling author. She's the mother of four and is pretty good at breaking up fights, or at least sending guilty parties to their rooms. She can't sing, doesn't dance, and despises tragedies, but she recently figured out how yeast works and can now make homemade bread, which she is really good at eating. You can read more about her and her books online at rachaelreneeanderson.com.

www.ingramcontent.com/pod-product-compliance
Lightning Source LLC
Chambersburg PA
CBHW070352130626
46556CB00007B/3143